BLACK
JACK
JETTY

Published by
MAGINATION PRESS
An Educational Publishing Foundation Book
American Psychological Association
750 First Street, NE
Washington, DC 20002

For more information about our books, including a complete catalog,
please write to us, call 1-800-374-2721, or visit our website at
www.apa.org/pubs/magination.

Cover and book design by Silverander Communications
Cover photograph by Westend61/Getty Images
Illustration on page 4 courtesy of Alex Forbes
Printed by Worzalla, Stevens Point, WI

Mixed Sources

Product group from well-managed
forests, controlled sources and
recycled wood or fiber
www.fsc.org Cert no. SV-COC-080730
©1996 Forest Stewardship Council

FSC

green
circle
USA

Library of Congress Cataloging-in-Publication Data
Carestio, Michael A.
Black Jack Jetty : a boy's journey through grief / by Michael A. Carestio.
p. cm.

Summary: Visiting his family's summer home on the New Jersey shore,
Jack begins to work through his feelings about his father's death in
Afghanistan and to find his place among the cousins and other relatives
he had never before met.

ISBN-13: 978-1-4338-0784-8 (hardcover : alk. paper)
ISBN-10: 1-4338-0784-X (hardcover : alk. paper)
ISBN-13: 978-1-4338-0786-2 (pbk. : alk. paper)
ISBN-10: 1-4338-0786-6 (pbk. : alk. paper) [1. Grief--Fiction. 2. Family life--
New Jersey--Fiction. 3. Seashore--Fiction. 4. New Jersey--Fiction.] I. Title.
PZ7.C21185Bl 2010
[Fic]--dc22

2010001260

First printing March 2010
10 9 8 7 6 5 4 3 2 1

BLACK JACK JETTY

A Boy's Journey Through Grief

by Michael A. Carestio

[signature] 6/8/19

MAGINATION PRESS WASHINGTON, DC

AMERICAN PSYCHOLOGICAL ASSOCIATION

For my girls,
Candice, Erica Lee, Riley, and Camryn

CONTENTS

TAKE ME HOME

"We have flown over the Rockies, across Nebraska, Iowa, Illinois, and a good portion of northern Indiana, and you haven't said a word, not a single sound, not even a grunt or a peep. Nada. Are you going to keep this up all the way to Philadelphia, Jackie Boy? Hmmmm. Wonder if I could get used to a solid month of peace and quiet down at the shore?"

What does she want from me? I told her how I felt. I don't understand why we have to leave home to stay a summer with people we don't even really know somewhere in New Jersey. I don't want to go. And I'm not going to like it.

Jack avoids making eye contact with his mom by keeping his nose buried in a book, *Galileo: The Great Astronomer.* When Mom gently tucks a stray strand of hair behind his ear, Jack shakes out his head, annoyed.

"I like your hair this long. It's very different than how you used to wear it."

Lots of things are different. I used to have a dad, too.

"A lot has changed. It's been one tough year for you and me, Jack. It won't be the same without your dad. No way that it could be. It'll take time, but we'll find our way. I think that spending time this summer with Dad's family will help us move on a little, and it will help them, too. They miss him, Jackie. Everybody misses your dad," says Mom.

"I don't know these people," Jack whispers, still not lifting his eyes to his mom's.

"I'm sorry. Did you say something? Did you open your mouth?"

"Suppose these people, suppose they don't like me?"

"They are not 'these people,' Jackie. They are part of our family. And you know them. What about all those stories Dad told you about all the summers he spent on Black Jack Jetty? You've seen pictures of that big old strange-looking house sitting practically right in the middle of the Atlantic Ocean. You have heard all about Uncle Black Jack. Remember the story about his pet sea gull, the one he taught to talk?"

"Birds can't talk," answers Jack firmly, still avoiding Mom's gaze.

"What do you mean birds can't talk? Of course birds can talk. What about a macaw? I've seen macaws interviewed on CNN," says Mom.

"A macaw can speak. But it can't 'talk' and neither can a sea gull. Talking or having a conversation requires intelligence far beyond any bird brain, Mom."

"Let me tell you something, Mr. Smarty Pants, lots of odd things have been known to happen on Black Jack Jetty. So if a one-legged sea gull wanders up to you on the beach this summer and asks what the Phillies did the night before, be courteous, and his name is Lucky. And what about your great Aunt Jane? You know Aunt Jane."

I met my Aunt Jane exactly twice. First, when I was three years old, my parents took me to Black Jack Jetty. I don't remember it, so I don't think it should count. The other time was at the funeral, and it was all a blur anyhow. I don't really know anybody anymore. It's just Mom and me now...Mom and me.

"You've got loads of cousins, aunts, and uncles who are dying to meet you," says Mom.

Oh great...them, too?

"They loved your dad as much as we did."

"Nobody loves Dad as much as we do," Jack says, looking straight into his mom's eyes. His chin threatens to quiver, his eyes turn teary.

Why am I scared? It's just a short trip. I don't want to be afraid.

"I bet Andrew and Cody can't wait to see the Atlantic Ocean live on their computers," says Mom. "I'm sure one day we'll go to Philadelphia and you can show them the Liberty Bell and Independence Hall."

"No big deal. They've seen all that stuff online before anyhow."

I promised Mom that I would Skype with Andrew and Cody every couple of days we're away. Andrew and Cody are my two best friends back home in Colorado. I'm hoping she forgets about it.

"It's not the same as seeing it with your own personal guide. You'll show them how to eat a cheese steak, and Aunt Jane will get tickets to see a Phillies game. Andrew and Cody have never even been out of Colorado for goodness sakes. They'll love it," Mom says, happy with her plan to keep Jack in touch with his base.

"We're not actually going into the ocean, right?" Jack asks.

"We'll teach you to ride the waves. I'm not saying we're going out far beyond the breakers, but we're good swimmers. I hear your cousins ride boogie boards and skim boards. Do you know what a boogie board is?"

"Something disgusting?"

"Very funny, Jack. A skim board is like a skate board only it skims across the water on the beach in about three inches of water. Not sure what you do with boogie boards," Mom says, smiling.

"Suppose we get caught in a riptide that pulls us out to deep water?" Jack says with all his heart.

"Nothing is going to happen," Mom says.

"That's what Dad said," Jack answers.

How can she say that? Bad stuff happens all the time, stuff that you can't ever be ready for. It's hard to feel safe again. I don't want to be scared. Funny thing, I'm getting used to the fear. How messed up is that?

Jack remembers the time when he took his dad to school, camouflage gear and all, for a show-and-tell. Jack's dad was in the Colorado National Guard. He always thought his dad looked awesome in camouflage gear. Everybody cheered. Jack even wore his hair in the same buzz cut as his soldier father. Jack was way proud of him. So, when his dad was called to active duty in Afghanistan, he told Jack to listen to what his mother told him. That she would always talk to him from her heart. Now she's asking him to go to a strange place and stay with strangers. Of course, he would do as she asked, but he didn't have to like it.

She looks at her son squarely in the eye. "Jack, I worry sometimes about what might come next for us, too. All this pain will take time to pass. At times it has been so overwhelming, more than I care to admit. I do know that I am not going anywhere. I know you're scared and you might be afraid you're going to lose me, too. And you've lost a piece of yourself in all this. I am hoping—no counting on the fact—that the love of Daddy's family, *our family*, and lazy summer days at the edge of the earth will help us feel a little more whole again. We can do this, Jack, I promise."

Mom hugs Jack tightly.

Just like Dad used to say, it is what it is.

CHAPTER 2

CALL ME JACK

"Thank you for flying with us today, and we look forward to serving you again real soon. Welcome to the City of Brotherly Love, Philadelphia," says the pilot over the intercom.

Jack is plenty worried as the plane touches down. He has never been this far away from home. He has never seen nor heard an ocean. He doesn't know this family.

I don't want to be here. Maybe if I throw up or something?

"Do you remember your cousins' names that are coming with Aunt Jane to meet us at the airport? Come on, honey, smile... please. It's going to be okay, really."

Mom is really trying hard to make this work. But I just want to go home.

"Nicky and Willie are the boys, but I'm not sure who's who. Nick is the older one. And then there's Allie," says Mom.

"She's the girl," says Jack, smiling.

"Very good, wise guy. There might be hope for you yet," says Mom giving him a playful shove. "Allison is Aunt Jane's daughter. Another girl cousin will be there, too. She's Riley. She's a little younger than you. But don't worry, she'll have no trouble keeping up with you boys."

Jack and his mom make their way toward the gate. "Kate. Kate," cries a tall, tanned woman.

"Aunt Jane," answers Mom, rushing toward her. They hug and kiss.

Jack spots two rambunctious young boys battling for position, a teenage girl, and a younger girl.

What a group. This is going to be the longest summer of my life.

"Hello, Jackie Boy," says Aunt Jane, giving him a bear hug and kiss on the cheek. "You are your father's son," she says, looking into Jack's eyes. "I'm so happy you both are here. Say hello to your cousins, Allie, Nick, Willie, and Riley. And there's a whole houseful of family dying to meet you down at the jetty."

Aunt Jane immediately rephrases her statement. "Everyone can't wait to see you."

"Look at you, Allie, you're beautiful," says Mom, repeating the bear hug and kiss routine. And then Allie hugs and kisses Jack.

"Now don't tell me who's who," Mom turns to the two still bumping blond brothers. "You're Willie. And you're Nicky."

"No, I'm Nick, no 'y,' and he's Willie with an 'eeee,'" says the taller of the two towheads.

"Close enough. I want you two to show Jack everything about Black Jack Jetty. We took him here once when he was much younger. But he doesn't remember much of that trip."

"Who's 'we'?" Nick asks.

"Jack's father and me," says Mom, placing her hand on Jack's shoulder.

Nick puts his eyes down, suddenly remembering what he knows about Jack's dad.

"I'm Riley," says a round-faced, brown-haired girl, extending her hand to shake Mom's, then his. She's no hugger, which is okay with Jack.

They all go to collect their bags. Jack didn't expect the airport to be so big, so busy, and so noisy. He is trying not to appear nervous.

"What's it like in Colorado? Is there an ocean near you? Are there beaches?" questions Riley.

"No ocean," says Jack. "But at *home*, we have lakes that have beaches. We also have fields and forests and mountains. Do you have those in New Jersey?" Jack says smugly.

"Well, kind of. We have the Pine Barrens," says Riley. "Creepy old trees. What do you do for fun?"

"Lots of things—we look at the stars, we go camping. Mom's favorite campsite is Rocky Stream Glen. Dad likes Eagle's Gorge," says Jack, wincing when he catches himself referring to his father in the present tense.

"You haven't seen stars until you see stars from Black Jack Jetty. Isn't that right, Aunt Jane?" says Riley.

"Yep, more stars than you could ever count," says Aunt Jane.

They arrive at the parking lot. "This is Dan's van. I like saying that. Dan's van," says Aunt Jane. "Dan is Nick and Willie's dad, and we borrowed it to pick you guys up."

"Shotgun," Nick shouts.

Willie pouts. And Nick climbs into the front seat next to Allie.

"You know about riding shotgun?" says Aunt Jane.

"My dad and I used to play it all the time with my mom," he says hesitantly.

"I knew it. There are so many things I can't wait to tell you about your dad. Jackie Boy is a great kid."

Was! He was a great kid! I don't want to hear any stories. I don't want to talk about him. Don't you get it?! My mom doesn't need to hear any more stories.

"Everybody has stories about Jackie Boy. Can I call you Jackie Boy or do you prefer Jack?"

"Dad always called me Jackie Boy. But can you call me Jack, please?"

"Jack it is," says Aunt Jane. "You know, old Uncle Black Jack was a Jack. He was certainly no Jackie or Jackie Boy. Can you imagine Black Jackie Boy Jetty? It doesn't have the same cachet. No, there are Jackies, Jackie Boys, and there are Jacks. But you, sir, to me are definitely a Jack. I miss my Jackie Boy terribly, Jack. And I know you do, too."

CHAPTER 3

DANGEROUS TREES

Aunt Jane, Mom, and Riley sit in front of Willie and Jack. Riding shotgun means controlling the radio. Nick is surfing station to station, until Aunt Jane threatens to "push the ejection button and launch him into the Pines." Allie is the driver. She talks on her Bluetooth while Nick makes faces at her. Aunt Jane is filling Mom in on the family. Aunt Jane laughs a lot. Mom laughs a whole lot. Willie doesn't say much. In fact, he hasn't said anything to anybody except to the well-stocked zoo—apes to zebras—he travels with in the van.

Jack looks out the window. "Boy, is it flat here," he says to himself.

Aunt Jane hears. "Well, Jack. New Jersey is called the Garden State, but it's getting harder and harder to find any gardens. And forget about mountains like you're used to in Colorado! South Jersey is flat, flat as glass.

"It once was once farmland, now it's mostly an interstate highway: suburban mile after suburban mile of fast food restaurants, gas stations, car dealers—new and used—strip shopping centers, convenience stores, and motels that advertise 'air-conditioning and cable TV,' until you reach the Pines."

"Like pine trees?" asks Jack.

"Yes, pine trees. Things might be different in Colorado, but in South Jersey pines don't rank very high among Mother Nature's best efforts. These pines are scrawny, desperate, and dangerous looking trees. The ground here is loose and sandy. Pine Barrens is an appropriate moniker for this thorny moonscape of Jersey wild that stretches to the sea," says Aunt Jane, looking out the window wondering how many thousands of times she's made this ride.

Great. Stuck in an ugly forest with dangerous trees and sand? I swear, when I grow up, I will never leave home. People who leave home don't come back anyway. I can be a park ranger, an astronomer, an inventor, or maybe a veterinarian. Anything but a soldier, and anyplace but New Jersey.

They drive for what seems like days to Jack. It's noisy with the radio blaring and people talking over each other to be heard. "Jack, are there wild animals in Colorado?" Willie asks.

"We always see deer and sometimes moose when we go camping. And sometimes whole families, a buck and all. There are bears and all kinds of birds and smaller animals like foxes and beavers."

"That's awesome," says Willie.

"The only mooses you'll see at Black Jack Jetty are Allie's boyfriends," cracks Nick.

"Ignore him, Jack," says Allie. "There are lots of things we can do down the shore, especially if you like nature. And of course there's lots of time for building sand castles, riding waves, collecting shells, chasing gulls, digging holes on the beach, looking for treasure."

"Yeah, there's a lot to do," says Riley. "You'll see."

"Smell that air, Jack? That's salt air," cries Aunt Jane, shouting over the blast of hot air that swooshes into Dan's van as she rolls down the windows.

Suddenly, Jack finds himself on a narrow thread of highway surrounded by dark water.

"You are smack in the middle of the Great Egg Harbor Bay, Jack. Three hundred years of providing the world with courageous fishermen and hardy partiers," says Aunt Jane. She looks out at the rolling bay as if it were the first time. Sleek waverunners skim the sparkling surface. Everything is moving in synch—boats, waves, reeds, and birds.

"Look at that egret, Jack," Aunt Jane says. "Look how graceful and delicate she is."

"I see her," says Jack. "Wow. I've only see them at the zoo."

"There's another one," says Willie. "I like egrets. I'll show you my feather collection. It's in my room."

"Look at the boats, Jack. That's called a marina," shouts Nick, looking at Aunt Jane, who in turn nods her head in approval.

CHAPTER 4

DOWN THE SHORE

The sign reads "Welcome to Margate City." Jack has never seen such a place. The city is super busy compared to his home town in Colorado. And there are people everywhere. It's packed with vacationing families.

"Who wants ice cream?" shouts Allie as she pulls up to a store with the giant head of a purple cow painted on it. "This is Udder Delight, Jack. Best custard down the shore."

He looks around to get his bearings. Udder Delight is in between small shops and stores selling bathing suits, beach toys, and sandwiches. It's only the end of June but the South Jersey sun is already in August mode, scorching hot. Jack's used to cooler mountain temperatures, so when he steps out of the van into the sauna, he gasps.

This is supposed to be fun?

Aunt Jane notices his reaction. "The humidity can take your breath away if you're not used to it. We'll get a stiff ocean breeze that'll blow it all out soon. What's your favorite flavor, Jack?"

"I like chocolate ...or vanilla...I like both the same."

"You're in luck, young Jack, for the specialty of the house is a vanilla-chocolate custard swirl. It's to die for," says Aunt Jane.

Again with the dying.

"Jimmies or no jimmies?"

"Eh, jimmies, please."

"One Jackie's Jimmies, please," says Aunt Jane to the girl behind the counter. "Sorry. Couldn't resist it, Jack," she says, handing him a cone.

"Oh, sprinkles," Jack says, pleasantly surprised, for he had no idea what jimmies were.

"Right, sprinkles," she smiles.

Jack smiles his first Jersey smile. He spots his mom, head bent backwards, looking up at something and pointing with her finger. He walks over and sees row after row of photographs on the ceiling.

"These are pictures of people who have been coming here for years and years. Here are all the Margate City lifeguards that ever were. I wonder who we might see?"

I know what's coming.

"There's your dad," Mom says, pointing to a tanned and muscled young man with his arms crossed against his chest. "There he is again."

"Jackie Boy was a lifeguard for three seasons. He looks pretty hot there," laughs Aunt Jane.

"I'll say," Mom agrees.

Can't we just go? Willie is eating just sprinkles, no ice cream. Let's pile back into Dan's van and get out of here, please?

"Allie! Allie!" shouts Aunt Jane. "Where's our driver?"

"I know where she is," says Nick, running around to the side of Udder Delight. "There she is." He points to Allie standing just under the purple cow's chin talking on the phone.

"She's always on her cell, talking and texting," says Nick.

"Teenagers," mumbles Willie.

"We call her Princess Cellular," laughs Nick.

"Allie!" calls Aunt Jane. Allie waves her mom off.

"I guess we lost our driver. She knows the way home. Everybody get back into Dan's van. Next stop is Black Jack Jetty. All aboard!"

Jack is glad to be back in the air-conditioned van. He looks out the rear window and sees lines of people the color of old pennies, lugging chairs, umbrellas, and bags. "Where are they going?" he asks Willie.

Without looking up from his animals, Willie answers, "The beach."

Aunt Jane heads away from the shops and stores. Traffic thins out. The houses are spaced farther apart. She makes a turn and the asphalt gives way to gravel.

When Dan's van stops, she says to Jack, "Behold the mighty Atlantic Ocean. And to your right is the brooding Great Egg Harbor Bay. Give each their due respect, Jack. Oceans are the most powerful force on earth. Pretty incredible, isn't she?" asks Aunt Jane."

Jack gets out of the van and forgets about the intense heat. Seeing and hearing an ocean up close and personal for the first time is an incredible moment. Crowned in white, the walls of grey-green water attack the shore in waves and crash on the black rocks of the jetty. Jack feels very small and vulnerable.

The waters are dark and move like a living thing. Nothing like the rivers at home, this water is different. It sways like the tall trees in the forest.

Jack stares at the ocean. He is mesmerized by the nature before him. A flock of sea gulls gliding overhead, their cawing alternately mocking and mournful, captivates him. Aunt Jane repeats, "I say the Atlantic is pretty awesome isn't she, Jack?"

"Yes, she is. How do you know the ocean is a she?"

"Duh. All great forces of nature are female. That's what Aunt Jane always says," interjects Riley.

"She goes on forever," marvels Jack. "I can't see the end of it. Kind of like the mountains at home."

"Speaking of home, welcome to Black Jack Jetty, your *ancestral* home," says Aunt Jane, directing Jack's eyes to the giant house looming before him.

"It's ours, too," add Willie, Nick, and Riley.

"That it is, cousins. She has survived hurricanes, nor'easters, and our family for eons. Nothing can hurt us here."

CHAPTER 5
BLACK JACK JETTY

Wrapped in porches and windows and turrets, the house is like a huge fortress holding the beach, clinging stubbornly to a vein of black rock that sticks into the Atlantic and Great Egg Harbor Bay like a ragged-jagged exclamation point.

Jack has never seen such a house as this one.

"This is open water and it's tricky and treacherous. People say the waters at Black Jack Jetty have an attitude, especially at high tide. If a swimmer isn't careful, these waves will flip you upside down, round and round, then deposit you on the beach thinking you've been run over by an elephant," Aunt Jane says.

"Is it really true Uncle Black Jack won the house in a card game?" Mom asks to change the subject.

"That was his story. That's how he got the name Black Jack. His birthday is July the eleventh, so he believed that he was born lucky. But Uncle Black Jack was born curious, too. He liked to fix things. He loved to make tools that solved problems. He built a drill bit that bit off more than other drill bits, making Uncle Black Jack a bit of a fortune."

"Jack likes to tinker around, too. Don't you, Jack?" says Mom.

"I'll show you Uncle Black Jack's workshop out back in the dunes. He called it his 'playhouse.' All his tools and designs are still there. He has 27 registered U.S. patents, you know," says Aunt Jane.

"Wow, 27?!" says Jack. "Can you show me his workshop?"

"Yes, sometime. But first, see that tower in the middle? The top is called a widow's peak and was built for sailors' wives to search the horizon for their men to come home. During World War II, Uncle Black Jack converted it to a fully equipped observation tower manned 24 hours a day by friends, family, and certainly by himself. He called it Nazi's Peak. He would scan the ocean for German submarines, and they were out there. If he spotted a U-Boat, Uncle Black Jack contacted the Coast Guard station down at Cape May on his ham radio. No enemies of the United States and Margate City were going to land on Black Jack Jetty on his watch," says Aunt Jane with considerable pride.

"Did he catch anyone?" Jack asks.

"No. But he came close once in the winter of 1944 when a Coast Guard Cutter responded to his sighting and chased the sub, even dropped depth charges. No wreckage was found so they figured it got away. It was in all of the newspapers, even up in Philadelphia. The boys will take you up there. The telescope and ham radio still operate. Who knows, that lost U-Boat just might surface again."

"Just a little shore lore," says Mom.

Aunt Jane takes Jack and his mom into the house.

"You know, Jack, to better understand what life here is all about, you've got to understand your great Uncle Black Jack," says Aunt Jane. "He swore the greatest character trait a person could have after honesty and compassion was curiosity. It was that curiosity that fueled his passion for invention and travel. During the winter months, Uncle Black Jack would go off to exotic places. But he always summered at Black Jack Jetty. He believed in second chances and epiphanies."

"What's an epi...epiph—"

"Epiphany," says Mom. "It's a moment in time when every-thing suddenly comes together. Uncle Black Jack believed you get out what you put in."

"Yes," Aunt Jane continues. "It is the putting-in part that is the toughest. Uncle Jack liked to look beyond the obvious. You know, Jack, you're named after him."

"I'm named after my father, Aunt Jane."

Aunt Jane winked at Mom. "And who do you think he and every other Jack in our family are named after?"

CHAPTER 6

THE FAMILY

It's been a long day for Jack and Mom. They are barely inside the house when people begin popping up from anywhere and everywhere. And they all want to see their Colorado family.

"I'm your Cousin Louis. These are my two brothers, Georgie and Peter. We used to share a bedroom with Jackie Boy. Whoa, the things we could tell you about your dad."

"You mean can't," corrects brother Pete.

"I'm Aunt Babe. I changed your father's diapers. He was a healthy baby, I can tell you that for sure."

"I'm Dan, you know, 'Dan's van.' This is my wife Nicole, and we're Nick and Willie's parents. I was a lifeguard with Jackie, your father. You can see us in the pictures on the ceiling of Udder Delight, the custard stand on Ventnor Avenue."

"Yo, Jackie Boy! I'm your Uncle Johnny. Put it there, nephew," a smiling man says, gripping Jack's hand firmly.

"Of all the boys, your daddy was the sweetest. Also the best looking. And you look just like him. I'm not technically your Aunt, but I've been a part of this family forever. I'm Sylvia."

"I tell you nobody went from first to third faster than Jackie Boy. Kid could fly. I bet you're fast just like your dad. I'm your cousin, Michael."

Jack's not used to being around so many people. He's not used to talking so much about his father. He's not used to these people. He's getting jumpy.

Get me outta here. Make it stop! What are they so happy about? Why aren't they sad? He's gone forever.

"Can I borrow my son for a moment?" says Mom. A couple of cousins have cornered Jack with yet more tales of summers past. Mom and Jack step outside and sit on the back deck facing the ocean. "And this is only some of the family. Wait until the weekend when the rest come. How are you holding up, buddy?"

"Okay. A little tired."

"Your dad used to swim out beyond the breakers. How he loved this place."

"Mom, I have to tell you something. I am sorry I invited Dad to show-and-tell. Maybe if I didn't, he wouldn't have gone to Afghanistan if everyone hadn't cheered for him in class. Maybe if it wasn't for that dumb show-and-tell at school, he would've changed his mind about leaving us. He didn't want to embarrass me. I made him come to my school and then he *had* to go to Afghanistan."

"Oh, Jack, you had nothing to do with your father's death. Not one thing!" says Mom. "Push out any guilt you might have. Let that go. Throw it out to sea. I'm glad your dad went to school and got to be with you that day. He told me how you introduced him to your class. How you explained his job as a soldier. How he beamed with pride. He was as proud of you as you were of him."

Jack stared at his mom. She always told the truth.

"Kate, can I see you a minute?" asks a cousin or aunt or friend through the screen door. "It's about that time you and Jackie Boy got stuck on the sandbar in the Back Bay with Don. Did you swim out there or did your kayak capsize? And where was Sylvia at first?"

Mom starts to laugh. "I haven't thought about that in ages."

"I'm good, Mom. You go."

Aunt Jane comes up from the beach and joins Jack and his mom.

"I think you're good and tired, young man," says Aunt Jane. "I'll take Jack to his bedroom, and you can tuck him in after you solve the mystery about who did what on the sandbar with Sylvia."

"Okay. You're in good hands," says Mom. "I'll be up soon."

Aunt Jane and Jack start the climb up what seems to Jack like several staircases.

"Thank you for your patience tonight, Jack. You were very polite and gracious with everyone," says Aunt Jane leading him up the great staircase. "It has to be hard to hear all these stories."

"They were nice."

"They were relentless. But they couldn't help it. Talking about your dad and all the good times is helping them deal with his loss. To me, talking about someone who's gone doesn't mean I'm not sad. How does it make you feel?"

"I don't know," says Jack. "Feeling better, I guess, or getting used to it. But why are they so happy?"

"Because they've been sad for so long. You see, happy memories can live with sad feelings. It seems strange, I know, but it is okay. And believe me, remembering happy times is not a betrayal of your dad. Quite the opposite, Jackie Boy. I mean Jack. Happy needs sad, and sad needs happy. I'm not making much sense, am I?"

"No, Aunt Jane, you are. And I think I get it," says Jack.

"Then you and your mother come, and everyone is so glad you're both here," says Aunt Jane. "It's like their Jackie Boy is back. We love him."

Finally, at the end of the hallway at the top of the stairs, Aunt Jane says, "Here's your room!"

Jack is sharing a corner bedroom with Nick and Willie. Jack sees that it has four windows, two that face the ocean and two that overlook the bay.

"Under a full moon, you can see all the way to France," jokes Aunt Jane. "Your father stayed in this room with his brother and cousins. They were great kids, each more handsome than the other. I wonder how many girls snuck…on second thought, we'll have that conversation in, oh, about eight summers."

"Look at this," she says, picking up a gold trophy sitting on a shelf. It is good size cup with two crossed oars. "Every year the lifeguards from Brigantine to Cape May hold races. One event is the two-man rescue boat—two miles out, two miles back. Your father and your Uncle Joey won it one year."

Jack takes the trophy from her hand. Hanging around it is a whistle. Aunt Jane removes it and places it around his neck. It's a silver whistle with a hint of rust.

"This is your dad's lifeguard whistle. When he left here to go to school in Colorado, he said that I should give it to someone who might need it one day. So here you are. This is yours now."

"Why do lifeguards have whistles?" says Jack.

"To get your attention. If you swim too far out, you'll hear the whistle. Everyone knows to look at the lifeguard when he blows the whistle. A lifeguard is like a police officer on the beach. He tells swimmers to move left or move right or come back closer to shore."

The whistle feels good around Jack's neck.

"Why don't you change into your pajamas, and I'll ask your mom to come up to say goodnight," says Aunt Jane. "I hope you enjoy your summer here, Jack. It's a wonderful place, you'll see. I'm so glad you and your mother are here. Oh, Jack, just one thing…it's not much, but it's important. Here on the jetty we try to tell the truth. And all feelings are real. And okay. Express yourself however you need to and I'll check in from time to time, too, just to hear how you are feeling. I love you, Jack. Sleep tight, your cousins have a big day planned for you."

Aunt Jane kisses him softly on his head.

Jack brushes his teeth and changes into his pajamas. The brothers hadn't come to bed yet. He was alone for the first time all day. He looks around the bedroom. This was his father's bedroom as a boy. It looks like a sporting goods store stocked with pennants, pictures, posters, and trophies—baseball, football, basketball, hockey, and swimming.

Jack tried playing football, baseball, basketball, and soccer. Didn't work out. Instead, Jack enjoys solving problems, figuring out how things work. He's naturally curious. He loves science, math, and computers. He likes collecting plants and bugs, and studying animals and stars. Jack and his dad would hike through the woods for hours collecting specimens. Jack cherished those times with his dad.

He cleans his glasses with his tee shirt to get a closer look at everything. In a team picture of a little league baseball team, Jack spots his dad not much older than he is now. His father was bigger and stronger and looked like an athlete. Jack looks in the mirror above the bureau...back at the picture...the mirror...the picture. No use. Jack is smaller, thinner, wears glasses, and looks more like a computer programmer than a centerfielder. *I'm no jock.*

Other photos show his father growing into the man that Jack knew. Jack couldn't hold in his tears any longer.

"Why are you crying, Jack?" asks Nick, dragging sleepy Willie in tow.

"I am not crying."

"Yes, you are," says Willie.

"Mind your business, both of you."

"Is it because you miss your dad?" asks Nick.

"Leave me alone. I hate it here!" Jack shouts. Jack pushes Willie down, and both boys start to cry.

Mom rushes in and separates the tangled-up boys.

"What's going on here?" says Mom.

"Jack pushed Willie," says Nick.

"He started it," says Jack.

"Started what?" Mom asks.

Jack says nothing.

"Jack, please. If you get upset, you mustn't hit or shove somebody. Now, tell Willie you're sorry. Go ahead."

Jack apologizes.

Mom tucks Jack in. "It's been a long day. Try to get some sleep. I hear there is a shell hunt tomorrow, bright and early," says Mom.

"Okay," says Jack. "Sorry about pushing Willie and yelling at Nick. It's just that they were teasing me."

"I understand. We'll do this together. We're in this together. I love you, Jackie Boy. Goodnight." Mom hugs him tightly.

"Now you two, into bed," says Mom to Nick and Willie. As she tucks them in she whispers, "He didn't mean it."

"I'm sorry, guys," says Jack again.

"It's okay," says Nick.

"I know. I'm sorry, too," says Willie.

CHAPTER 7
MOVING ON

The next morning Aunt Jane and Aunt Eileen arm everybody with a bucket.

"Time for our sea shell collecting expedition!" yells Aunt Jane. "Participation is mandatory."

"Last one to the beach is a rotten egg," jokes Aunt Eileen.

Jack jumps right in, asking his two aunts loads of questions about what types of animals live in the shells on the way to the beach. As he scours the beach and tide pools for shells, he watches sandpipers, tiny brown birds that scurry on spindly legs, dancing with the surf and feasting on tiny sea life deposited on the beach by the waves.

Over the next couple of days, the cousins play hard at digging holes, building sand castles, playing all kinds of ball, flying kites, chasing birds, riding waves, and watching huge clouds fly high in the sky.

One afternoon, the waves begin kicking up as high tide comes rolling in, lots of white water crashing on the beach at super speed. Perfect for body surfing. All the cousins are in the water riding, dodging and diving under the ferocious waves. All the cousins except Jack.

"Jack, why aren't you riding waves?" It is his teenage cousin, Allie.

"I don't know how," Jack answers.

"It's time you learn," says Allie and takes him by the hand toward the ocean. Jack stops. "I don't want to go in," he says.

"Oh, yes you do. Trust me. You're just afraid because you don't know how. I was afraid until my mother taught me how to handle the waves."

"Aunt Jane taught you?"

"Yeah, my father wasn't around much."

"Where is your dad?"

"In Philadelphia. They're divorced. He travels a lot for his job."

"That's must be hard for you," Jack says.

"It is. I used to get angry with him for not being there. What am I saying? I still do, but less and less. It is what it is. There's nothing wrong with expressing how you feel. Your feelings are your feelings, you know? It's just that eventually the anger has to pass and you have to move on."

"At least you can call your father on the phone, I can't," says Jack.

Allie looks at her cousin, feeling his sadness. "I'm not saying divorce and death are the same thing, Jack. I'm just saying that I understand how you feel not having a dad around."

Jack looks up from the sand, smiles slightly, and asks, "Show me how to ride waves?"

Allie shows Jack when to turn sidewise and jump just as the white water hits, avoiding the full impact of the wave. She teaches him to go under the waves.

"Jack, as the wave approaches, dive under the white water and you will pop up behind it. It is an awesome feeling. Try it. It washes away everything."

The first time he does it, it feels amazing. The water whooshes over him.

Then Allie tells him how to body surf. "It's all about timing and the kick!" she shouts above the roaring surf. "Get out in front and point your arms, hands, and fingers at the beach and let the wave propel you forward. It's really wild!"

Jack swallows a lot of salt water, but by the end of the day, he is twisting and turning in the surf, riding waves with his cousins. Now he is laughing as the waves dump him hard on the sand.

Aunt Jane and Mom are standing on the beach. It is the first time Aunt Jane has heard Jack laugh.

"Well, look at that," smiles Aunt Jane. "This just might work, Kate."

"You know, he has nightmares. He dreams that we're both going to get blown up like Jackie. Loud noises can frighten him. But right now, right now he looks just like a normal kid riding waves," says Mom.

"He is a normal kid," says Aunt Jane. "He just needs to ride this out. He will, you know."

Aunt Jane takes off to the ocean.

"Yo, Jack, check this out," shouts Aunt Jane, diving under a charging wave.

"Hey, wait for me," shouts Mom as she quickly joins her family in the familiar waters off Black Jack Jetty.

CHAPTER 8

TREASURE HUNT

"My mom looked for it and couldn't find it," says Nick. Willie nods in agreement.

"My...my dad searched for it, too. He told me," Jack says.

"Everybody's mom and dad and brother and sister have searched for Uncle Black Jack's hidden treasure room. We're going to find it," Riley states, slapping her fist into the palm of her hand.

It was the end of June and it had been raining for five consecutive days. Down the shore, five straight days confined to indoor activities can feel like forever. "Five successive rainy days is a recipe for mischief," warns Aunt Jane to anyone who will listen.

Riley, Jack's eight-year-old cousin with opinions, puts into play Uncle Black Jack's hidden treasure. Tall for her age, Riley can run as fast as any of the boy cousins. She is naturally curious and not at all bashful about asking questions or taking charge.

"How do you know it's a room and not a treasure chest buried in the sand?" Nick asks.

"We're too close to the water to bury anything valuable in the sand. Besides, once you bury treasure you can't look at it or add to it without people getting suspicious," says Riley. "My parents are police officers so I know all about things that are suspicious. It has to be in the house, maybe behind a hidden wall, a secret door, or maybe it's not a whole room but something like a chest in the widow's peak. We'll start in the peak and work our way down. Try not to be too conspicuous," Riley cautions.

"What's that mean?" Willie asks a rare question.

"It means don't let them notice what we're up to. Be *incon*-spicuous and keep a low profile. Act natural," says Jack.

"Right," says Riley. Nick and Willie nod in unison.

How are we supposed to hunt for hidden treasure without attracting attention in a house full of bored people? That's like getting on a bus without your pants and hoping no one notices.

They spend the next few rainy days knocking on walls, lifting carpets, moving pictures and furniture, opening crates, and measuring interior spaces to make sure that they match up with the exterior.

They search from the widow's peak to the cellar of the great house. Nothing.

They start over and search everything again.

The treasure hunters gather on the porch to discuss their next move.

They go over everything again. They already have searched that house high, low, and in-between.

"We need a plan," says Riley.

"We've searched everywhere," says Nick.

"We've searched everywhere two times," says Willie.

"We've searched everywhere everybody else searched," says Jack.

Riley nods in agreement.

"We need to be different. We need to think out of the box," continues Riley.

"Maybe we need to think out of the house," says Jack.

"I think I need an ice cream cone," says Willie.

Everyone agrees with Willie. Hunting for treasure is hard work. So the cousins don their ponchos and make for Udder Delight by way of the beach. The ocean is really rough. Ferocious waves blast the dunes, building walls of creepy brown bubbles that slide silently toward them.

"What's that stuff?" asks Jack.

"Sea foam," says Riley. "The waves churn up the sand like cake batter. The winds whip it up the beach. It's pretty cool." She scoops up two fistfuls of foam and blows it away. "Go ahead, try it. Don't be afraid, it won't peel your skin off," she teases her cousin. Jack reaches down deep into the bubbly brown mix and tosses the foam into the wind.

"It's sandy," he says.

Even ice cream can't solve their dilemma. The cousins, looking for help anywhere they can find it, turn toward the pictures on the ceiling of Udder Delight for inspiration. They see a picture of Uncle Black Jack himself standing next to a giant tuna he caught in a long-ago tournament. They see another of Uncle Black Jack with a baseball player. There are lots of photos of Uncle Black Jack. They study all the photos for clues.

Then Jack sees his dad and smiles a little. Looking at the photos of his dad made him feel good this time. He drifts off thinking about his dad—their camping trips and nature hikes, setting up the telescope and looking for craters on the moon, his dad tucking him in at night. All the good stuff. Riley's urgent plea brings him back.

"Where is your treasure room, Uncle Black Jack?" demands Riley. "Really, now. Give us a sign!"

"We've looked everywhere," says Nick.

"Obviously not or we would've found it," snaps Riley.

"Maybe it's not in the house," says Jack.

The cousins stop talking and look at their Colorado cousin.

"I mean, the whole family has turned that house inside-out just like we did and nobody has found it," says Jack. "Maybe it's not there."

"Wait. Are you saying Uncle Black Jack's treasure doesn't exist?" says Riley in a serious tone.

"I didn't say that."

The cousins stare at Jack like he has three heads.

Riley slowly says, "Yes, there is a treasure. Everybody knows there is a treasure. Uncle Black Jack wrote a letter to the family clearly saying that there is hidden treasure at Black Jack Jetty. You're new here, but we know the story. Ask Aunt Jane if you don't believe us. She'll show you Uncle Black Jack's letter."

"My dad believed there was a treasure so I believe there's a treasure. I'm saying maybe it's not in the house, that's all."

The rain slows to a steady drizzle. It is still windy, and a white mist is coming in from the sea. Jack takes his vanilla-chocolate swirl cone and turns toward Ventnor Avenue, walking back to Black Jack Jetty.

"Don't be such a shoobie," chides Nick.

"Only shoobies walk on the street eating ice cream," chimes in Riley.

"A shoobie?" asks Jack.

"Shoobies are...they're like tourists. They come for a week or two and do goofy vacation stuff like playing miniature golf on the boards on a Saturday night," says Nick.

"Shoobies are not cool," adds Riley. "We go back to the jetty by the beach."

And that's what the four cousins do. No shoobies in this group.

"Shoobies," says Willie. "Shoobies."

"He likes saying it," says Nick.

They walk along in silence, wolfing down their ice cream, with visions of buried treasure dancing in their heads.

"What do you think the treasure is?" Nick throws out to the gang.

"Gold bars. Maybe jewels," suggests Riley.

"Money, I bet it's money, piles of it," offers Nick.

"Stuff from his travels around the world," adds Jack.

"Pictures of us," says Willie.

"What kind of treasure is that? Uncle Black Jack's been dead for a million years, how could he have pictures of us?" mocks Nick of his younger brother.

Willie turns away and goes off chasing sand pipers. Jack joins him, running after the tiny birds dancing with the dying waves on the glimmering sand. Heavy storm clouds are quickly gathering in the western sky, and the wind is beginning to howl off the ocean.

"We better pick it up," warns Riley. "Looks like another storm is coming in fast."

Jack looks out at what used to be the horizon. A black curtain is heading right at them. "What's that?" Jack says.

"That's rain," shouts Nick over the screaming surf.

A bolt of white lightning fires up the dark sky. The cousins run for cover from pelting by rain and salty spray that stings their faces, eyes, legs, and arms.

CRRAAAACCCCCCCCKKKKKKKK

Jack grabs his ears and, losing his balance, stumbles.

CRRAAAACCCCCCCCKKKKKKKK

"Willie!" shouts Nick to his younger brother.

CRRAAAACCCCCCCCKKKKKKKK

"Jack!" shouts Riley. She runs back and grabs her cousin by the arm. "Run to the playhouse!"

They crash through the door of Uncle Black Jack's playhouse. Breathless, they fall to the floor in drenched heaps.

"Everybody okay?" asks Riley. Nick and Willie nod their heads. "Jack?"

"I'm alright," he answers, not convincing anyone.

CRRAAAACCCCCCCCKKKKKKK

Jack jumps up, ready to run to who-knows-where.

"Thunder can't hurt you," says Nick. "But lightning can burn you up like a burnt bagel."

"That's true," says Willie.

"Well, we can't get struck by lightning in the playhouse," Riley says.

"No, but lightning can strike the playhouse, set it on fire, and we'll get burned like a burnt bagel," says Nick.

"Can you stop with the burnt bagel stuff, please?" orders Riley, making a face at Nick and rolling her eyes toward Jack.

"Oh, right," says Nick begrudgingly.

"I'm okay," Jack says again, actually almost meaning it. "I never heard thunder that loud in my life."

The four cousins collect themselves.

"So this is Uncle Black Jack's playhouse. Jack sees a hand-written sign. "Joie...joie...de...viv...vivre."

"*Joie de vivre*," says Riley. "It's French. It means 'love of life.' That was Uncle Black Jack's motto."

Jack scans the room. It's an awesome sight. There is a huge wooden workbench that bears the scars of countless nights that Jack imagined Uncle Black Jack spent banging and twisting out an idea until it made sense. The walls in the work area are covered floor to ceiling with pegboard from which are attached tools of every description—screwdrivers, wrenches, hammers, drills, calipers, gages, brushes, pliers, saws, and several odd looking pieces no one can identify.

Uncle Black Jack's playhouse is pretty much off-limits to kids. Aunt Jane herself would occasionally come here, but kids are not allowed without a grown-up. But kids being kids, they would sneak in now and then to see what goes on here, always careful not to disturb anything, for if Aunt Jane learned that you had been in there, you'd better fess up.

Suddenly from near the workbench, Willie cries out, "Houdini is gone!" The startled cousins jump up from the floor. "Houdini has escaped again," mourns Willie, holding an empty round cage.

"Who's Houdini?" Jack asks.

"His hermit crab," answers Nick. "Why did you keep him in here? I thought he was in our bedroom."

"He's safer here. Nobody comes here," Willie says.

"Last summer, Willie's hermit crabs kept getting out of the cage because when he feeds them, he doesn't like locking them in, so they crawl up the side and push the lid up and get away. Aunt Jane said the escaping crabs reminded her of Houdini, a famous magician. Willie calls all of his hermit crabs Houdini."

"Do you always find them?" asks Jack.

"Sometimes we do. Sometimes Aunt Jane's cat, Holly, finds them first," Nick laughs.

"That's not funny," shouts Willie, taking a wild swing at his brother.

"Sorry about Houdini, but we've got bigger fish to fry, like finding hidden treasure," says Riley firmly and without much compassion for Willie.

Willie is already on all fours, scouring the floor of the playhouse for Houdini. The treasure will just have to wait as far as he is concerned.

The three remaining treasure hunters huddle together.

A lightning bolt lights up the playhouse like a space shuttle launch. Jack tries not to notice.

"Burnt bagel," says Nick. Riley elbows him in the ribs.

"We've searched everywhere but here," Jack says, determined to focus on treasure and not thunder.

"Here? In the playhouse?" asks Riley. "There are only three

walls, there's no attic and no cellar. Where could Uncle Black Jack have put it?"

The side door to the playhouse opens and in come Aunt Jane and Mom wearing yellow ponchos. "What's this all about? Is this an off-site meeting of treasure hunters?"

Riley takes the lead. "We ran in here to get out of the rain. It was really raining buckets, Aunt Jane, honest it was."

"And what are you doing on the floor, William?"

"Houdini escaped," says Willie.

"You know about the treasure hunt?" asks Riley meekly.

"Everybody knows about the treasure hunt. We've all been on the same treasure hunt."

"So you believe it exists?" asks Riley.

"Uncle Black Jack said it exists so it exists," answers Aunt Jane. "C'mon, let's go, you're not supposed to be here, but I'll make an exception because of the storm."

"What about Houdini?" whines Willie.

"Tomorrow morning we'll come back and look for him. He's in here somewhere, there's no place to go," promises Aunt Jane.

The rain has let up a bit and they all head back to the house.

"It's almost a full moon, and there's a high tide around midnight all week. Throw in this storm and the waves at Black Jack Jetty will be kicking," Aunt Jane says.

CRRAAAACCCCCCCCKKKKKKK

Down beach, a blue streak of lightning strikes somewhere. Jack clutches his mother's hand tightly.

Nick smiles. "Don't even think about saying it," Riley warns her cousin.

CHAPTER 9
WAVES WITH ATTITUDE

With a break in the rain, everybody flees from the house like it is on fire. Most go to the boardwalk, some to Udder Delight to gawk at shoobies. Jack is upset about how upset the thunder had made him. He asks his mom if he can stay home and maybe talk with Andrew and Cody. That is fine with her. She'll stay home, too. And that is fine with Jack.

Though the rain stops, the wind does not. There is also a wet and heavy mist that casts Black Jack Jetty in a ghostly glow under the new moon. Jack is alone in his bedroom on the computer with his friends in Colorado. They tell him about their camping trip to Utah with the Nature Club. He tells them about learning how to ride the waves and all about hunting for Uncle Black Jack's secret treasure and Houdini's escape. The boys make Jack promise to tell them right away if they find any treasure or the missing hermit crab.

He comes downstairs and sits with his mother on the front porch.

"How are Cody and Andrew?"

"Good."

"Are you having fun searching for the treasure?"

"I am but its hard work."

"Your great Uncle Black Jack had a unique personality. Do you know that he would lie out on the beach at night and take a 'moon bath'? He believed that soaking up the moon beams increased his creativity. So the idea of hidden treasure would certainly appeal to him."

"Did you search for the treasure?"

"Yes, one foggy night with your dad."

"In the house?"

"Up in the peak."

"Didn't find it?"

"Obviously not. You know, Jack, Dad and I would sit right about where we are now, taking it all in, especially the sound of the waves smashing into the jetty. He loved to swim out beyond the breakers. He was fearless. I saw him save a man twice his size once. How do you like the ocean so far?"

"It's alright."

"He found peace here. I know you're angry. Everyone who loved him was cheated when he was killed."

I don't care about anybody else. I care about us.

"Can I go to bed, Mom? I'm really tired."

"Okay. I'm going to sit here awhile more. It's a full moon to-night, but you can't see much of it because of the clouds. I'll be up to tuck you in, in a bit."

Jack climbs into bed and is sleeping before he hits the sheets.

CRASSSHHHHHH

Jack shoots straight up in bed, eyes and mouth wide open, an explosion. He looks over at Willie and Nick, still sleeping. The posters, pennants, and pictures are undisturbed. That is about the realest dream he's ever dreamed. When will it stop! He closes his eyes and falls fast asleep.

BOOOMMMMMM

Jack jumps right out of bed this time. It sounds as if a freight train has run right through their bedroom. Unbelievably, Nick and Willie sleep through the whole wreck.

He opens the bedroom door and looks down the long hallway. It's empty. Could it be no one else heard it? Jack goes to the bedroom next to his where four of his older cousins—Peter, Liam, Tom, and Anthony—are all snoring away. It is so real. Yet no one else hears anything.

I must be going nuts.

Jack returns to his room and climbs back into bed.

BAAAMMMMMM

This just can't be a dream!

Jack tries to fall back asleep. Willie and Nick are not pretending—they are sound asleep. He wants to call his mother, but he doesn't. He grabs his cell phone to call Cody and Andrew back home, but he doesn't. He is scared to death in his father's old bedroom. He pulls the covers up tight and hides his head under the pillows, praying for the explosions to stop.

BOOOMMMMMM

BAAAMMMMMM

CRASSSHHHHHH

Make it stop!

The mornings after a storm down the shore are sweet and pure. The beach is smooth. The cloudless sky is a brilliant blue. It feels like the dawn of time. The sun is high. All the cousins are up early. Jack says nothing about the explosions from the night before.

I must have been dreaming. I don't need anyone thinking I'm crazier than they already do.

The sun is hot. The water is super rough, and a fierce riptide and whistle-blowing lifeguards keep swimmers out of the ocean. The cousins do beach stuff—volleyball, Wiffle ball, football. Some build sand castles. Willie chases sandpipers. That night almost everybody goes to the boardwalk. They go on the rides, play games, and eat cotton candy. They are tired as they walk back to Black Jack Jetty by way of the beach. The moon is full, casting a white stream over the storm-tossed waves. Jack goes to bed that night with a good feeling.

CHAPTER 10
I BELONG HERE

CRASSSSHHHHH

Not again.

This time Jack doesn't move, hoping this will make him invisible. After what feels like forever, he finally turns ever so slowly to the brothers, still sleeping in their beds.

ROAAARRRRRR

He leaps out of bed, surrendering his invisibility. The room is lit by four beams of light pouring through the windows.

BOOOMMMMMM

Are we being bombed? Why is everyone still sleeping? Why aren't they scared like me?

BAAAMMMMMM

That's right outside. He creeps toward the window and peeks out. The beach and jetty are as bright as day. The water shines like diamonds in the full moonlight. The wind is whipping up the waves into a foaming frenzy.

There is no one there.

CRASSSSHHHHH

He clasps his hands over his ears. No good. The explosions tear through his fingers.

This must stop. Jack runs from the bedroom, storming through the sleeping house out onto the back deck, confronting the angry waves.

BOOOMMMMMM

Jack is angry. Jack is crying. He stares hard at the ruthless waves. He puts his dad's lifeguard whistle to his lips and blows it as hard as he can, over and over again, over the screaming surf.

"Make it stop. Make the waves quiet. Make them stop now. I'm afraid! I'm afraid! You owe me that!"

Jack stops blowing the whistle. He bends over in exhaustion, when he hears someone whisper, "What are you doing?" He turns to see Riley sitting in a rocker on the deck. Jack feels embarrassed and angry. No one was meant to see him.

"Who are you yelling at?" she continues.

"What are you doing there spying on me?" Jack demands, wiping away his tears.

"I'm not spying on you. I was here first...taking a moon bath."

"A moon bath! That's the dumbest thing I ever heard. Just some dumb girl-thing?"

"Dumb girl-thing! A moon bath is no different than a sun bath or a water bath. Everybody knows moon baths are healthy for you, especially under a full moon and a star-filled sky like tonight. Besides, old Uncle Black Jack always took moon baths. But you wouldn't know that being a stranger."

The word hung in the moon light like a dagger. Riley wants to take it back the moment she says it, but the damage is done. She leaves the porch and retreats into the house.

"I'm not a stranger! I'm Jackie Boy's son! I belong here!" Jack shouts to the stars.

To Jack's astonishment, the surf shushes. The waves keep roaring in and crashing against the rocks of Black Jack Jetty as they have done forever. But Jack doesn't hear them. It is as if someone hit the mute button or pulled the audio plug on the raging sea.

He turns to see if Riley has come back, maybe she hears the silent waves, too, but he is alone. Under the full moon, Jack watches the waves and looks up to the stars, all the while clutching his whistle.

They could be the brightest stars I've ever seen.

After a while, Jack drifts off to his room, and then drifts off to sleep, feeling less afraid and more at home than he has for a long time.

CHAPTER 11

HOUDINI DOES IT

Early the next morning, just as the sun is rising, Jack makes his way to Uncle Black Jack's playhouse. That same morning Riley tells Aunt Jane about the previous night's encounter with Jack on the deck. "Who was he blowing the whistle at, Aunt Jane? There wasn't anybody in the water."

"I think I know. By the way, you should strongly consider apologizing to Jack for calling him a stranger. This is his house as much as it is ours. He's family."

"I know. I'll apologize," agrees Riley.

As Jack approaches the playhouse, he is rested and relaxed. The night had produced no more horrible dreams, explosions, or terror. The huge waves driven by the storms pounded the jetty, roaring through the night at high tide under the full moon, yet Jack slept through it all. He had found peace last evening on the beach.

Jack stands quietly in the center of the playhouse. He's looking and listening for Houdini, just like he and his father searched for animals back home in the forest. He thinks again that this playhouse is a pretty awesome space. He could definitely spend more time here.

What's that?

Jack stands perfectly still. There it is again. A scraping sound that could be Houdini's claws dragging his shell across the concrete floor of the playhouse.

Follow the sound and I'll find the crab. I'll put Houdini back in his cage and place him on Willie's bed so he'll see his pet first thing when he wakes up.

Jack lies down to get a crab's eye view of the floor, searching under furniture and equipment. The sound is coming from the rear of the room, the section built into the sand dune.

"There he is!" Jack shouts to himself, spotting Houdini's red shell, painted like a Phillies baseball cap, slipping behind the pegboard wall before Jack could reach him. Jack sticks his fingers under the wall, vainly trying to reach the runaway hermit crab. Instead, his fingers find a piece of metal, like some sort of lever, and the tool-covered wall slowly swings open.

Jack stands up and steps back. He is anxious to say the least. The swinging wall reveals a doorway. The crisp morning light exposes a room about the size of a walk-in closet. There are bookshelves and a round table on which rests a shining box.

Uncle Black Jack's hidden treasure room! He's found it. He's also found Houdini crawling under the table. Jack's heart is about to jump out of his throat. He doesn't know what to do. He grabs his dad's lifeguard whistle around his neck and starts blowing. He runs out of the playhouse to get his cousins and runs smack into Aunt Jane and Mom.

"Jack, what's wrong?" asks Mom.

"I found it."

"You look like you are about to burst," Aunt Jane says.

"I found Uncle Black Jack's hidden treasure room!" he blurts out. Jack takes his mom's hand and leads them back into the playhouse.

"Cheese and crackers," whispers Aunt Jane looking into the open door way. "It really does exist."

"Of course it does," says Jack.

Aunt Jane's eyes go to the shining box. "Looks like stainless steel. Uncle Black Jack's material of choice." Lying on the table in front of the box is an envelope.

Behind the table is a shelf on the rear wall and on it are some pictures. Holding Jack's hand, Mom picks up an ancient photo of a young soldier, a World War I American solider. He is wearing two medals, the same two medals on the shelf.

"He looks just like your dad," says Mom.

"It's Uncle Black Jack. He does look like Jackie Boy. I've never seen him this young before. Wow," marvels Aunt Jane.

Jack reaches for the medal with a blue ribbon and a silver star, then stops.

"Go ahead, Jack, pick it up," says Mom. He holds it in his hand. "It's American." He picks up the other, a bronze shield with a gold ribbon. "This one is French. Both are for bravery."

At that moment, Riley, Nick, and Willie rush into the playhouse.

"Aunt Jane?" gulps Riley.

"Houdini!" cries Willie, lunging into the room and retrieving his beloved hermit crab.

Riley and Nick watch Willie run into a small room. Then they see the steel box.

"Oh me, oh my! Is this…" asks Riley.

"I think it is," answers Aunt Jane.

"We found it," says Riley.

"Actually, Houdini found it. I found the secret lever," says Jack.

"Good work, Houdini," proudly says Willie.

"Who's that?" asks Nick pointing to a framed picture of an old time baseball player wearing a pin stripe uniform and "New York" across his chest.

Mom takes the photo off the shelf and reads the inscription. "'To my pal, Black Jack, the King of Atlantic City.' It's signed Babe Ruth."

Aunt Jane sees something else on the shelf—a silver lifeguard's whistle and a white feather, perhaps from a sea gull. She smiles. Precious things.

Everybody is talking at once, excited at the discovery of the secret room.

"What's in the box?" asks Riley. "Open the box, Aunt Jane."

"I think we should open the envelope first," says Aunt Jane. She begins to read out loud.

"'Congratulations. You've found the treasure. If you're reading this, chances are that I am gone. No regrets. It's been a great life. And because into each life a little rain must fall, hopefully the contents of this box will help to ease the concern that rainy days often bring. The idea is to take only what you need and replace it when you can, so others who come after can reap the benefits of our family. I wonder who you are. Do I know you? Or have you yet to be born as I write this? Just curious.'"

No one speaks, but every eyeball in the room is focused on the sparkling box. It was most assuredly crafted by Uncle Black Jack himself. It has a single clasp in the center which Aunt Jane gingerly unfastens, allowing the lid to slowly open. Music! It's a music box...a song from the 1930s, "We're in the money. We're in the money. We've got a lot of what it takes to get along!"

"Sense of humor that Uncle Black Jack," says Aunt Jane.

In the box are 11 gold coins and a slip of paper. Aunt Jane picks up a coin and examines it. "It's ancient. There's a head on the coin that looks like a Roman Caesar. And it's gold. It's real gold."

"I knew there was gold. I just knew it," crows Riley.

"What's that piece of paper say, Jane?" asks Kate.

Aunt Jane removes the white slip of paper and unfolds it. "It says 'I-O-U,' somebody has been here before us and left with one gold coin."

"What's I-O-U mean?" asks Nick.

"It is literally a promise to repay a debt. 'I owe you'," explains Mom.

"Who left it?" asks Jack.

"Whoever wrote it didn't sign it," Aunt Jane says. "They didn't date it either."

"It's a mystery," Riley says.

CHAPTER 12

THE BEST OF SUMMERS

Word quickly spreads across Margate City about the discovery of Uncle Black Jack's treasure room. The cousins become local celebrities. A picture of Houdini even makes it up on the ceiling of Udder Delight. Decades of past treasure hunters come to Uncle Black Jack's playhouse to congratulate the four cousins as well as to see the secret room that had eluded them.

As promised, Jack Skypes his pals Cody and Andrew back home. He sends video of the treasures, of his cousins, of Houdini. He'll see them soon with more stories of Black Jack Jetty.

The next few weeks are blissfully uneventful. The water warms up, and Jack is fast becoming a big boogie boarder. Next summer he'll be an even better boogie boarder.

Willie still doesn't lock Houdini's cage, but the wily hermit crab hasn't made a break for it and seems to be basking in the limelight of his celebrity.

Nick is working on his teasing skills, with Princess Cellular and Willie being the leading targets. In between moon baths, Riley decides that over the winter she'll attempt to solve the mystery of the I-O-U found in the steel box.

Spending this summer with Jack and Kate has helped to ease Aunt Jane's pain over the loss of her beloved Jackie Boy. Watching the cousins come together is a great sign for the family, she decides.

Late one afternoon, a couple days before they are to return to Colorado, Mom and Jack are walking on the beach when she asks him about blowing the whistle and shouting at the waves on that moonlit night.

"You were asking your dad for help, weren't you?"

"I was afraid. I felt alone."

"You know when Uncle Black Jack took leave of this earth, they threw a huge party for him. Everyone shouted 'Joie de vivre' and leaped into the Great Egg Harbor Bay with their clothes on in tribute to him. Uncle Black Jack led an extraordinary life full of family and friends. He certainly marched to his own drummer, and he lived by a set of rules that usually gave people the benefit of the doubt. And to no one's surprise, he left Black Jack Jetty to his favorite niece, then just 16 years old."

"Is that Aunt Jane?"

"Yes. Uncle Black Jack knew she would use this place to keep the family together, somewhere to celebrate life or as a refuge from the storm. Black Jack Jetty is home. That's what your dad thought, too. And I've come to think that also," says Mom. "Black Jack Jetty keeps us all connected."

"I'm okay now, really," says Jack. "I know Dad hasn't left us. He's in my heart. He's in yours. He's here at Black Jack Jetty. I'm not afraid anymore. Dad doesn't owe me anything, you know."

Jack smiles and hugs his mother with all of his might. She buries her face in his hair. He smells like sunshine on a bright sunny day during the best of summers, down the shore at Black Jack Jetty.

NOTE TO READERS

There is no doubt that the death of a parent is immensely painful and the feelings surrounding your loss are very strong. No one can replace your mom or dad, and you can intensely feel that something is missing in every part of your life for a really long time. When you're grieving, you may not know what to do or what to say. You may not know how you should feel or what you should think. But what exactly is grief? How do you feel? And what can you do to take care of yourself and your feelings during this difficult time?

WHAT IS GRIEF?

Grief is an emotional response to loss. Your grief might make you feel nervous, worried, or scared. You might feel angry or guilty. You might feel overwhelmed or feel numb, like nothing has happened. Or you may feel all these emotions in confusing or mixed-up ways. While these feelings are common to someone who is grieving, everyone reacts in different ways when they have lost a parent.

HOW DO YOU FEEL?

When you are grieving, your feelings can be deeper and stronger than they have ever been before and can last a long time. Understanding why or how you feel the way you do can help you help you feel better sooner.

Sad. When kids are grieving they can feel very sad. You miss your mom or dad, the time and activities you shared, the feeling of connection you felt, and even times that you won't be able to spend with your parent in the future. Sometimes kids are afraid their sadness will overwhelm them, like they might start crying and not think they will be able to stop. Or they may try to avoid feeling sad at all.

Numb. Sometime kids feel nothing at all, like they are numb, when they expect to experience strong feelings of sadness or loss. They kind of just shut down or turn off. Feeling nothing when you think you should be feeling something can be confusing. And sometimes it makes kids feel guilty when they don't feel anything. If this happens to you, don't worry too much. Your mind is likely trying to protect you from feelings that are too strong for you to feel all at once. Your feelings will come back when it is safe for you to experience those feelings.

Angry. When kids are angry, they might yell or scream. Or sometimes the anger will come out in other ways—you might be irritable or not so patient with others. Sometimes grieving kids are so angry that they misbehave or break rules on purpose. If you are feeling angry, you are reacting to the big loss you feel and the difficult changes it means for your family. Anger can also be an unconscious (out of your awareness) way to keep sadness, anxiety, or other painful feelings away because anger might feel safer or easier to express than these other feelings. It's like the anger is unconsciously protecting your from more upsetting emotions.

Anxious. Some kids can feel anxious and scared following a parent's death. Kids may worry that something bad could happen at any time, making it difficult for them to relax and enjoy life. Older kids may especially worry about the remaining parent, becoming anxious especially when they see him or her crying or worried. Your anxiety comes from a very basic concern, such as "Who will take care of me if something happens to the parent I still have?" You can ask your parent about this because all kids (even those who haven't lost a parent) need to know that there will always be a loving adult to take care of them.

Guilty. When a kid is grieving, it can be really hard to feel happy. Many kids feel guilty about enjoying life when their

mom or dad is no longer here to enjoy it, too, or when the sur-
viving parent is still very sad. Kids can feel guilty, too, if they
believe their (normal) angry thoughts about the parent some-
how caused the death. Kids need to know that their thoughts,
wishes, and anger had nothing to do with their parent's death.
When these feelings stick around, they can turn into feelings
of guilt. Remember, guilt never helps anybody. Neither of your
parents would want you to feel guilty. All parents want their
kids to enjoy and embrace life.

WHAT CAN YOU DO?

There are things you can do while you are grieving your parent's death. Dealing with your grief in positive ways doesn't
mean you don't care or love the parent you've lost. It doesn't
mean that you have forgotten your mom or dad or how much
your parent means to you. With the support of your family
and your own positive actions, you can find ways to cope with
your very deep loss that will ease the grieving process.

**Keep in mind that grief is a normal response to death and
that grief is a process.** This can be very difficult to remember
especially when your feelings are so strong and your hurt is so
deep. Getting used to what is missing from your life and how
things aren't the same after your parent dies is difficult. But be
aware that, with time, these strong feelings will get smaller and
you should begin to feel better and happier. Remember, grief is
a process and it takes times to go through. Most kids find the
first year the hardest and the second year much easier. During
the second year, kids slowly start to feel more like themselves
and back to normal even though they of course still think a lot
about and miss their mom or dad.

Be with friends and family. When you are sad, you might just
want to be alone. This is common and lots of kids act this way.
It is also common to act out grief feelings by being irritable,
angry, or impatient with friends. Some kids who are grieving

find it very hard to do the things they used to do, and some people become angry with others, even though they never used to feel that way. But after a while, try to get back to your routine and hang out with your family and friends. Being around people could help you feel better and they understand that this is all very difficult for you.

Try to talk with others if you can. There is no pressure to talk about your parent's death. Some kids find this helpful, others do not. Your parent will likely bring this up with you and may even ask if you have questions about your mom or dad's death or death itself. Other relatives, family friends, teachers, or neighbors may also provide a listening ear and can be a good support system during this time. Sometimes just talking about what you are going through can help you to sort out your emotions. Your friends and siblings (especially older kids and teens) are also a helpful resource, too.

Keep doing what you like to do. If you like to play soccer after school, keep doing that. If you read a lot, pick up another book. If you like playing computer games, do that. Anything that you enjoy to do is positive and useful. This can help give you a sense of security and stability at a time of major change.

Remember, don't try to forget. When you lose someone you love, try to remember that person instead of trying to forget him or her. You could remember all the ways your mom or dad showed love to you. You could think about what that parent taught you. You might even do some of the activities and hobbies you enjoyed doing with your parent. It might make you feel sad, too, but remembering will help you feel connected to your mom or dad, and ultimately will ease your feelings of loss.

Look to memories. Keep your parent's memory alive in a variety of ways. You can display photos of your parent and the whole family together. Make a scrapbook or a photo album with pictures and mementos of times shared. Plant a tree or garden in the parent's memory. Talk about memories of your parent in everyday conversations like "Mom would have loved that movie, don't you think?" or "I can really throw the football just like Dad."

Talk to yourself. Lots of kids find it helpful to coach themselves through difficult feelings and situations. This is called "self-talk." You might say to yourself when you are feeling bad, "I'm feeling sad now, but I can talk to my mom about this and I'll feel better later" or "I feel so angry about dad's death, but I can try to write about my feelings or draw what I'm feeling and maybe that will help."

Be prepared. Certain places, times of the year, birthdays, or holidays may trigger an emotional reaction that reminds you of your loss. Don't be worried too much if this happens, but be ready when it does. For example, if you know that your first Thanksgiving without your mom is coming up, talk to your dad about it. Maybe your dad can think of something you can do to remember your mom and try to make the day a bit easier for everyone. Maybe you can light a candle in your mom's memory or write a poem about her. Inviting a friend or neighbor to join you and your dad for dinner might also help.

Understand that dreams and nightmares are common. It is not unusual for kids to have dreams and even nightmares following the death of a parent. Sometimes these are "happy" dreams of doing something fun together with your deceased parent. Those kinds of dreams can actually leave kids feeling quite sad because for a few moments after you awaken, the dream can seem so real. Then there is the very sad and upsetting realization that this was "just a dream" and the parent in the dream is no longer alive. These dreams can be quite upsetting, in part because they can feel so real while you are having them. Other dreams are quite the opposite but also upsetting because they have strong "negative" themes in them, such as aggressive or scary images or very sad themes of the parent's death or funeral. It helps kids to realize that while both of these kinds of dreams or even nightmares can be quite disturbing, they are not uncommon. You have just been through a very intense, sad, and painful experience, and your dreams are a reflection of that. Remember that even the most upsetting dreams are your mind's attempt to work through all the hard feelings, images, thoughts, and experiences that you have endured. It can help to talk about the dreams with an adult you trust rather than keeping them inside. In addition, you can journal about or draw what you remember from the dream, or how you felt in the dream or about the dream. If these dreams persist, it can be a sign that it would be useful to see a counselor to get some help with the feelings you are experiencing.

Get more help. After the death of a parent, many kids are helped considerably with books such as this one and the suggestions above. However, if your feelings are too strong and overwhelming, or if you are having lots of problems at school, at home, or with your friends, you may benefit from getting extra help or counseling. Talk to your parent or another trusted adult. They can arrange for you to speak to a professional therapist or counselor who will help you find additional ways to deal with your loss.